VITAMINS FOR THE MIND®, SERIES 1

OVERCOMING YOU!

The Journey of Joe Braxton's Fall and Rise to a Corporate Idol

ROBERT C. MCMILLAN

McMillan & McMillan Books

PORTFOLIO
Published by McMillan and McMillan Books,
(a division of The McMillan Group, LLC)
McMillan and McMillan Books (USA) LLC, PO Box 249
Highland, Maryland 20777, U.S.A.

First published in 2008 by Portfolio,
a member of The McMillan Group (USA) LLC.

LIBRARY OF CONGRESS CATALOGING IN PUBLICATION DATA
McMillan, Robert C.
Overcoming You! The Journey of Joe Braxton's Fall and Rise to a
Corporate Idol / Robert C. McMillan

ISBN – 13: 978-0-9817759-0-6
ISBN – 10: 0-9817759-0-X

Printed in the United States of America

Contents

Acknowledgments

Many people have come across my life in the business and personal environment that have inspired me to write this book of inspiration, hope and dreams. This book is for those that have shared personal stories of going through storms and overcoming corporate, family, health and life challenges to find success in the eye of the storm. This book is to inspire those getting ready to go through a storm, in the process of going through a storm, or perhaps have just gone through a storm.

In addition to the thousands of people I have met throughout my career who have had a profound impact on my life, I would like to thank two significant contributors to the development of this book in particular—Maynard McAlpin and Willie Jolley.

This book would not have happened without the direct influence of my grandfather, James G. McMillan and my father, Larry A. McMillan.

Finally, deepest thanks to my wife and two children for their support and understanding, for each hour I took from them now goes to you.

Introduction

This cross-generational story about the battle with our internal Super-Ego is full of practical principles, life balance techniques and self-empowerment tools which will inspire and motivate executives, managers, and employees within corporate, private and government industries, as well as students at all levels, to perform at their maximum potential.

This is the story of Joe Braxton, a successful business executive who, for a long time, skated through Corporate America never performing at his maximum potential. You see, Braxton was a fast talker with a golden tongue who out smarted people much of his career by doing just enough to get by, making the right decision at the last second, or being in the right place at the right time.

You may be wondering what is wrong with this picture. Braxton was like many of us, conditioned to only meet expectations, avoid any risks and resist stretching to exceed goals. This is commonly referred to in the industry as sandbagging, setting goals so low that they hardly require any effort to accomplish.

The fact of the matter is that there are two types of people: those that are conditioned to doing just enough to get by and those that perform at their maximum potential to change their condition. Braxton chose the path of doing just enough to get by.

Braxton is a product of the new American Dream generation. The old American Dream to own a home "someday" isn't enough for the X, Y and Z generations. Oh, no. The new American Dream is, "Get It All Today."

Braxton dressed in the finest suits, drove a BMW luxury sports car and ate at four-star restaurants. On the social scene, Braxton thrived on charisma and loved the spotlight. The guy from high school who couldn't fight his way out of a paper bag broke through the corporate glass ceiling and wanted everybody to know it.

Braxton was able to work his way up the ranks at McBracey Enterprises, going from a management level position to an executive officer level of the company over a five-year period. His rise to the top is not as important to understand as is his near death from success and fall from grace.

Over his years with McBracey Enterprises, Braxton developed relationships, institutional knowledge and power and control which resulted in an inflamed Super-Ego. Braxton came to work when he wanted to and left when he felt like it. Braxton was a master at managing strategic projects and getting things done while shielding himself from mistakes at the expense of others.

Over his years with the company, Braxton was able to give the illusion of walking on water, exceeding expectations and deliverables, by cleverly using others as stepping stones beneath his feet. But he miscalculated what was exactly enough to get by when his previous boss was replaced by a new boss, Mrs. Johnson, with her own agenda to clean house. His world crumbled when she demanded more out of him and his team and exposed him to the pack of corporate wolves.

The reality is, Braxton represents characteristics in us that we either suppress or allow to flourish. He is a constant reminder that we are all accountable for how we end the race in life, but not necessarily responsible for the tools we start the race with. He reminds us that our real work in life begins when we realize we do not live by the Super-Ego to obtain a social-class status, a certain economic level, the American Gangster Dream, or for the "Bling Bling," but that we ultimately live by the person inside each of us, our Conscience. Until we discover that the Super-Ego is the road block that impedes us from reaching our maximum potential, we will struggle in making our aspirations and dreams a reality. "Overcoming You!" is a story about the battle between the Self-Conscious, Conscience and the Super-Ego that exists inside every boy, girl, man and woman illustrated through Joe Braxton.

Self-Conscious is defined by the dictionary as *a consciousness of ones-self, ones-being*. Conscience is defined as the voice that tells you the difference from right and wrong and it monitors and guides your decisions, actions and behaviors. I like to refer to this as the first voice.

Super-Ego, on the other hand, is defined by the dictionary as *an inflated feeling of pride in your superiority to others*. My definition of this is slightly different: I like to refer to the Super-Ego as the second voice that suppresses the Conscience right or wrong decision filter and ignores guidance, resulting in inflated pride and the feeling of superiority over others.

The balance between the Conscience and Super-Ego is Will. Will is defined as the power of control the mind has over its own actions (the freedom of the Will). Understanding the four definitions of Self-Conscious, Conscience, Super-Ego and Will, one could agree that the Conscience and Super-Ego can be ignited from the internal Will, which I like to refer to as the *Will Factor* because Will is directly related to and viewed as the first cousin to the Conscience and Super-Ego. The Conscience and the Will Factor can work hand in hand to manage the Super-Ego. The purpose of the Will Factor is to support the Conscience and help it to overcome the odds and assist in accomplishing great dreams and aspirations in life. However, the Super Ego works against the Will Factor, and Conscience working alone to create the attitude of superiority, self centeredness and comfort, in turn devouring the Will and Conscience instinct to perform at your maximum potential.

Braxton's life seemed to end when his previous boss resigned and he was fired by his new boss, Mrs. Johnson, who was brought in from a Fortune 500 company to turn things around. But, you will discover how his death was resurrected into new life the day he became the boss over his Super-Ego.

This cross generational entertaining story of practical principles, life balance techniques and Self-Empowerment tools will inspire and motivate executives, managers, individual contributors and the next generation of leaders (kids, teens and youth) to perform at their maximum potential in life.

One
"Braxton, You're Outta Here."

The door swung open behind me.

"Braxton, the gig is up!"

I turned slowly, annoyed from being interrupted from the BrickBreaker game I was playing on my Blackberry, and looked into the furious eyes of Mrs. Jackie Johnson, the new vice president of McBracey Enterprises.

"Excuse me," I replied, for my team was in the middle of completing the strategic merger and acquisition project she had requested.

"You heard me," answered my boss, slamming the door behind her as she entered the room with a Human Resources employee. "We're through with you. We are consolidating your team under another department. I have asked you over and over again to arrive at work during core hours, submit quality products and be sensitive to urgent issues requiring executive resolution. Over the last 90 days I have tried to work with you, coach you and transfuse some ambition into you, but your blood just won't take it. I have tried every management tool on you, but to no avail. A person like you needs to be hit by an eighteen-wheeler before you learn to look both ways before crossing into the corporate express lane. Quite frankly, I nor this company cannot afford that kind of liability. So I'm giving it to you straight, Braxton. We are eliminating your role and transitioning you out of the company, so take this 52-week severance and get on with your life. This company is done babysitting you. You'll receive your final check two weeks from today's date with severance. Braxton, this is your last day with McBracey Enterprises. You're fired! Have a good life."

Mrs. Johnson turned and asked the Human Resources person, who was also new to the company, if she had anything to add. With a smirk on her face, she looked at me and said, "We'll be in touch."

And Mrs. Jackie Johnson and the Human Resources person left the room.

Two
Life's Perspectives

I sat, dumbfounded, holding my Blackberry and looking at the BrickBreaker game still running on the screen. I thought, this new executive team has been in place only 90 days. I can't be the issue: they are the issue. They don't understand what it takes to get things done around here. "They're out of touch," I exclaimed, pounding on the desk and screaming at the top of my lungs.

Out of habit I resumed playing BrickBreaker on my Blackberry and contemplated my next move. I wondered if I should contact my lawyer? A friend of mine told me that anytime you get a visit from Human Resources they should get a visit from your lawyer. He used to say, "They screw with me, they see my lawyer in the morning." That's what he said every day until they finally fired him. He spent a fortune on attorney fees.

As the Washington, DC afternoon sun spread across the table, I got up to close the shades. I kept hearing Mrs. Johnson screaming the words, "You're fired, Braxton." Her voice became louder and louder in my mind.

I fell to one knee and my soul uttered the words, "Fired? Fired Again?" This was the fifth job I had been fired from.

I began to think about my wife and kids. How would I support them? Pay the mortgage, the bills, college tuition? You see, once I climbed the corporate ladder I told my wife she didn't have to work anymore. She could be a stay-at-home mom taking care of four children in the home we owned.

I stood up in rage and yelled, "Fired?" I screamed, "You can't fire me after all I have done for this company, after five years of service." I yelled at the top of my lungs the dumbest thing I had ever said, "You can't fire me because I quit."

And then it hit me, I'm getting severance, 52 weeks of severance that they are paying me not to work here anymore. What possible better deal can you ask for than that, I thought? I quickly retracted my statement about quitting and peeked through the blinds to see if any Human Resource people had overheard me. At that instance, feeling relieved, I walked over to my computer, grabbed the mouse and opened my music download folder to play a song that would reflect the mood of the evening. This called for a celebration song because I felt like I had hit the lotto.

I played the "Cha Cha Slide." I had just learned the dance moves from a company picnic and turned up the computer surround sound, jumped on my office desk and danced like I was in a Britney Spears MTV video.

After dancing for about ten minutes I thought, good riddance. This wasn't the first time I had been fired. Getting fired didn't matter much to me. There are millions of corporate jobs out there and I could talk my way into any of them. That's how I had gotten this far, and if they fire me, I'll just go and get another six-figure job. This was my philosophy. Why should I be loyal to a company and perform at my best when the company is not loyal to me? If they can fire me at anytime, why should I give them the best that I have to offer? Why perform at my maximum capacity? I never claimed to be the best, nor did I ever want to be the best. I just wanted the check. I had my own philosophy of life. I called it PNPL (Play Now Plan Later).

And this was my philosophy:

Living but only once, we must get everything we can now, later for the future. Get it now or die trying. All of what? Satisfaction, money and pleasure! And what is pleasure? "Living life to the fullest and leaving nothing for later, getting all you can get by any means necessary, partying the night away, being in the in crowd, the inner circle, and having a network that spans multiple countries" was my motto.

And what about work?

Sure we have to work, but make the money, don't let the money make you.

For no company pays a person what he is truly worth—so just produce based on what you are paid. If you are paid peanuts, then produce peanut deliverables. Why work harder than you have to? So work just enough to cover your expenses and increase your chances for a raise, bonus or incentives.

But be no slave to your boss—live full, die empty!

See, life will pass us by just as it has done to the World War II and Baby Boomer generation, stripping the loyalty from their hearts and leaving them to live off of a penny pinching pension and a bankrupted social security fund.

No, not me, not this X and Y generation. I say get yours by any means necessary, for when we die we are dead a long time.

So live the life while the living's good, worry about tomorrow later.

This was my mindset and thinking—my philosophy on life. For I am a product of the X and Y generation.

What about service? Service to others?

Service comes with a price tag and that's why every political servant is compensated. There is nothing free in life, so you do nothing for free. This is, of course contrary to the values and beliefs of previous generational philosophies and in direct conflict with what my grandfather taught me years ago. This was my philosophy on life.

Three
The Death of a Rich Man
and the Birth of the Super-Ego

My grandfather was born in 1915, during World War I and he did not have access to the opportunities we have in this day and age. He was not a rich man, but worked honestly to take care of his family. He managed to put all five children through college. He was a genius during his time, given he was the inventor of the financial float. He would borrow from one creditor to pay off the debt of another creditor, just as our capitalist society does today. He floated money from one creditor to another, then to the local grocery stores and gas stations, just as the world economy is run today. He had tabs all over town, worked hard, and paid his debts. The only asset he owned was an intangible asset, called his good name.

My grandfather was from the South and earned his living as a custodian and carpenter. When he died, I questioned my grandfather's philosophy, for what did a good name and credibility get him in the end? He dedicated his whole life to his family, job and others with no reward in the end.

The day I got fired from McBracey Enterprises was a pivotal moment in changing my philosophy. I was forced to reflect on my grandfather and all the things he used to tell me about life. I observed first hand my grandfather's work ethic. From childhood through my teenage years my parents would take my brother and me down south to spend the summer with both sets of grandparents. My brother would often stay with my mom's side of the family and I'd stay with my dad's.

When I spent the summers with my grandfather he would wake me up every morning at five o'clock, tip toeing in my room and whispering in my ear, "The early bird catches the worm," as he went off to work.

I would jump up and get dressed to go to work with him, but by the time I was dressed he had already driven off.

When he came home, I would ask him why he always left so early in the morning. In his soft tenor voice he would explain that every morning millions of birds, all competitors, wake up and search for food to survive. He said that 50 percent of the birds were eaten by their predators because they did not have enough energy or strength to defend themselves, and 50 percent of the worms died because they were caught by birds. So, it doesn't matter if you are a bird or worm, in the morning you "better have your nose to the ground."

Just as he left for work with energy and passion, he would return home, but on the days when he was not able to find that golden worm, he would say, "The darkest hours of day are just before dawn," signaling that the work day was over and he had not been successful or happy with his progress or performance that day in meeting the needs of his family. "But joy cometh in the morning," he concluded.

Whether he was well compensated or not, he always performed at his best and was optimistic about life.

When he died, I asked myself what he had gotten in the end for all his hard work, good name and deeds to others. He had let his conscience lead him in everything he did and it left him penniless. I thought the joy he talked about never came in the morning because his time ran out before a change could come. That's the day I gave my life over to my Super-Ego. I loved my grandfather deeply and vowed I would never live that way, and I would let my Super-Ego lead and my conscience follow. That was the day I changed my philosophy on life—and buried my grandfather and laid conscience along side of him in the coffin.

Four
It's Not You Against the World,
But It's You Overcoming You

After the emotional reminiscences of my grandfather, my pride screamed, "To hell with this company. I don't need you, you need me." If they don't want me, then good riddance! I'll take the severance and be on my way."

Angrily, I began to pack up my briefcase to leave the building forever but suddenly I became weak. A heavy weight on my back wouldn't let me move, and a deep unexplainable depression entered my soul, forcing me to sit down. I thought I was having a heart attack, but little did I know this was the beginning of the battle between my Super-Ego and Conscience.

My mind began to play back clips of me and my grandfather sitting on the back porch of his home in North Carolina. I tried to turn it off, but I couldn't. It kept playing over and over in my mind.

I grabbed a bottle of water and poured it on my face to calm my nerves. After regaining my composure, I realized this was my Conscience that I buried years ago coming back to life, but my Super-Ego tried to kill it each time it raised its body from the coffin.

I realized I was having an out–of-body experience just like I saw on the Oprah Winfrey Show. In a twinkling of an eye, I was standing over three people looking down on them, my Conscience in a coffin, Super-Ego and I, standing in the middle of both of them. My Super-Ego began yelling and holding down my Conscience as it tried to get out of the coffin. As I watched from above, my Conscience threw my Super-Ego back with one arm and got up out of the coffin and said to my Super-Ego, "You ruined our name and creditability. You threw it all away."

Then my Super-Ego stood tall and told my Conscience that nobody in this day and age lives based on a good name, except for credit scores. You've been dead so long, I guess you wouldn't have known that. After all, your grandfather had a good name all his life, and what did it do for him or his family? For he was too good, too kind, too honest to take a nickel even if he had earned it. And his good name is worthless to us, for it cannot be liquidated into an asset," my Super-Ego screamed.

At that moment I saw a figure come out of my body. I was now looking down on four people. I couldn't make out who the fourth image was.

Suddenly I heard the voice of my grandfather calling my name as if he were there in the office with me. I could hear him singing a song my grandfather used to play by Al Green. Terrified, still in the out-of-body experience, I got up to try to snap myself out of this. Pinching myself, I walked back and forth pacing the room as my grandfather's voice came through the walls, louder and louder.

There was a brief pause, and the last words I heard my grandfather say that day were words he said every morning, "Lord, thank you for another day to right my wrongs." At that point the fourth image walked back into my body.

My Conscience said to Braxton, "We have another day to right our wrongs." My Super-Ego quickly jumped in to challenge my Conscience as I stood listening. "Joe, we just need to take the severance and find another job man, another sucker. Why spend time trying to right wrongs and mend broken hearts? If you do that, chances are you'll be the one left holding the broken heart in your hand. If the bridge is out, baby, take another route. Don't waste time fixing a bridge. Build another one, and for the bridge that is burning, let the next person who crosses it worry about putting out the fire. As a matter of fact, we should let it burn so no one else can cross it! I mean come on Joe, why should someone else gain as a result of your sweat and labor," said my Super-E

In that moment I stood, saying nothing and allowing my Super-Ego to overthrow my Conscience once again. I heard my Conscience plead,

"Joe, don't let him do this to us. Please, you have another day to fix this. It's not too late, the best in you is yet to come."

At that moment Joe Braxton ignored his Conscience, choosing again to follow the Super-Ego, for after all it was what had gotten him this far in life. The sky began to darken and suddenly all of the figures vanished.

Five
Rebirth of the Super-Conscience

With the Super-Ego back in charge of my thoughts and actions, my philosophy of life was unchanged. In fact it was stronger than before, probably because of the encounter with my Conscience. I realized I was no longer in the out-of-body experience, so I embraced my philosophy and began to strategize on how to get another job while keeping the severance deal! I sat thinking, it would be hard plowing, finding another gig.

My references were against me. But I'd been fired before. I was a good actor in interviews, saying all of the right things and doing just enough to get the job.

I laughed mirthlessly.

On the computer I pulled up my network of recruiters and associates I had developed relationships with and began to send out emails for opportunities in the industry. After all, I figured a 52-week severance package would be even nicer if I could double my income by finding another job. My Super-Ego led my thoughts, and I toasted myself that evening with, "Here's to a better job, an easier and higher paying job."

Hearing footsteps in the hallway, I glanced out the window and then realized the darkest part of day was upon us. It was almost dawn. At that moment I heard the footsteps of the janitor walking by my office to turn off the final set of lights on the floor and collect my trash before retiring for the night. As he walked into the corner of my office, I glimpsed the side of his face. Something was different about him, his height, complexion and age.

I got up out of my chair to get a closer look as he bent over removing the trash from the can. When he turned in my direction, I realized it was my grandfather standing right before my eyes. In amazement, I saw he was dressed in the same clothes he wore to work when he was alive.

Little did I know this would be the beginning of the death of me, my Super-Ego.

The following is what my granddad said to my Super-Ego that killed it and changed my life forever: As I approached my granddad with open arms, I yelled "Pop Pop," the name I always called him. He replied, "Sir, I do not approve of you but I do approve and love the person inside of you. The person trapped inside of you is my grandson, of my name, value and cloth. But you, Sir, are the Super-Ego spirit that I ran out of my life years ago."

"Yes, I recognize you, Super-Ego, a corner cutter, a gifted talker, an impressionist of a hard worker, and a person who would trade his good name for material gain and pleasures. Yes, I recognize you very well. But I say to the person inside of you, Joe Braxton, remember a name is the only thing that you can take with you to your grave that will live forever here on earth. Buildings crumble, nations fall, but a good name always stands firm."

He continued to say, "I sacrificed my life to show you the value of a good name but, more importantly, the insignificance of material gain and pleasures of the world. But you have proved my philosophy wrong. I am sorry I failed you with my lesson and caused you so much pain."

Confused, I stood listening to him. I wondered why he was apologizing to me. Then he turned and walked out the window into the night, uttering his final words, "The darkest part of the day is just before dawn; Lord thank you for another day to right my wrongs."

In that moment I ran after him screaming, "You were right; you were right!" But it was too late. He was gone. Crying and feeling that I had disappointed him, I saw my reflection in the window. I looked closer and closer and instead of the reflection of one man I saw three images in the window before me—myself, my Conscience and my Super-Ego. I stood astonished, wiping the tears from my eyes.

The three images began to wrestle and fight with one another aggressively. As I watched, I saw one of the three figures punch the other right in the nose. It was me, Joe Braxton, punching, kicking and beating my Super-Ego. Then I heard Joe Braxton's loud inner-voice with power and conviction screaming to my Super-Ego: "Braxton, you're fired!"

"Get out of me!" I answered, "I am going to bury you once and for all. I don't know you anymore. I'm through with you now and forever. Flee from me and never enter again. You have insulted my grandfather and ruined my life. I will not let you ruin his good name."

As the clouds covered the sky, I saw Joe Braxton and my Conscience put my Super-Ego in a casket and bury it.

At that point, the room calmed, and as I looked through the window only one reflection remained: it was me, Joe Braxton, and the other images had vanished. I began to see a bright white light coming toward me; closer, closer and closer it came. And then darkness was all around me.

Six
The Transformation of Life

"Braxton, Braxton, get up!" I turned my head over on the desk.

"Braxton, get up!" The glare from the sky hitting my face, I sat up, my eyes still closed. I was sweaty and clammy from passing out at my desk and sleeping in the chair overnight.

I heard a voice again, "Braxton, get up!"

And I realized it was my Conscience calling my name. My transformation was complete and my Super-Conscience was born.

I got up and ran over to the window to see if the images from last night were still there. I could see only two images from the tinted glass and they were me and my Super-Conscience, for we had killed and buried my Super-Ego.

At that moment I took accountability and control over my own life. Looking at both images with stern eyes, I said, "There is a new boss in town and his name is Joe Braxton. We are going to do things differently. No more cutting concerns, saving your best for a rainy day and getting over on life. We are going to follow this 4 Point Performance System:

And the two of us took this oath that day:

- Follow my conscience, never allowing the resurrection of my Super-Ego.
- Rebuild my name and credibility for the next generation.
- Perform at my maximum potential each day as if it were my last.

- Thank God for each day, for each day is an opportunity to do what I couldn't do yesterday!

As we completed the oath the images faded away and the only image that remained was Joe Braxton, and this was the beginning of my new philosophy and battle for success.

As I turned to walk back to my desk to plan my next move, the door opened. In walked Mrs. Johnson and the Human Resources employee.

Mrs. Johnson exclaimed, "I see, Braxton, you have not taken orders once again. You still haven't packed. Didn't we communicate that you were fired yesterday? She asked are you wearing the same cloths"?

I looked at her with a new smile and described to her my out-of-body experience. I explained to her that I had changed my philosophy on life and taken on a new lease. She laughed and said, "Braxton, we are on to your games, and it's not going to work this time."

The Human Resources Generalist handed me the termination letter, which included a 52-week severance package. I opened the envelope and saw the check had already been written. The Generalist indicated that all she needed was my signature agreeing to the separation. As I stared out the window contemplating what to do, I saw the images reappear in the window. My Super-Ego had resurrected itself. My Super-Ego said, "Braxton, sign the paper, fool. Take the money, run." As Braxton started to sign the paper, my Super-Conscience jumped into action, and I witnessed my Super-Ego and Super-Conscience in a violent battle. As I stood watching, my body language projected what I was seeing in the tinted window, although Mrs. Johnson and the Human Resources Generalist thought I was having a nervous conniption. In the twinkling of an eye, my Super-Conscience picked up a samurai sword and cut off my Super-Ego's head.

As my Super-Ego's head lay on the ground, I heard the Generalist calling my name, "Braxton, Braxton," she screamed, "I am talking to you."

I looked from the tinted window back over to the Generalist and Mrs. Johnson and said, "I respectfully decline your severance package." I tore up the check and resigned, effective immediately.

They looked puzzled. At that moment I politely walked out the office never to return to begin living my new philosophy on life.

Seven
What Doesn't Kill You
Can Only Make You Stronger

As I placed my key into the lock and entered my home, concern and fear overshadowed me. I was unemployed without any source of income. I did not want to tell my wife or children because I did not want them to worry. So I cooked up a story for them. When they greeted me as I walked through the door, I told them I would be working from home from now on because of the cost reduction efforts at the company. I told them I was given the option to work from home like many of the other employees in order to reduce the office space, in turn reducing the real estate costs.

As I walked into my home office, I thought of all of my friends and networks I had developed over the years. Surely, I thought, they could help me get a job.

Over the next several weeks I worked my way through my Rolodex, contacting associates, friends and recruiters, never letting my wife and children know I was unemployed. My goal was to find something before it became obvious.

As I talked to my friends, I told them about my out-of-body experience and new philosophy of life. But when I talked about my new philosophy, there was complete silence.

As the weeks progressed, I no longer received phone calls or invitations to the inner circle social parties. Old friends stopped calling. My network dwindled from over 500 people to no one.

On my own, I was able to talk my way into several interviews with local companies but soon I realized that my name and references were against me. When talking with recruiters I found that many of them had already done their research on my background, and they had reached their own conclusions about me. It seemed as though the closer I got to a job, the farther the job ran away from me. I seemed doomed to failure. I thought I would never find someone to give me a fresh start.

Within the course of six months I was all alone, in a state of depression and at the lowest level in my life, contemplating suicide. I began to question my new lease on life. Life challenges were beginning to take a toll on me in the worst way.

Eight
Got Faith?

Because of my old philosophy on life, I lived every day for pleasure. I saved money for a rainy day but not rainy months. Over the last several months, I had just about drained all of my savings account and 401K retirement fund to support my family and pay the mortgage. On my 180th day of being unemployed, we were two months away from being homeless and were forced to live on tuna and sardines.

That day, I had to sit down with my wife and our children, one eight and the other six years old, and tell them I had lost my job. I had to tell them that I had been unemployed for six months. I told them all about the battle between myself, my Super-Conscience and the Super-Ego, but that didn't stop the tears when I told them we were on the verge of bankruptcy. That was the hardest thing I ever had to do.

My oldest child looked at me and asked, "Daddy, why did you quit your job?" I said no, Daddy didn't quit his job. Daddy was given a choice to stay the same person and never reach his maximum potential or to change to reach a level of greatness. Daddy decided to change, and sometimes change comes with sacrifices that impact everyone." My youngest child said, "Well how much does change pay?"

We all laughed, holding each other. I said, "Change makes you rich in many ways."

And I was praying for a change for the better in my job hunt. I realized that change was not free. There is a substantial price to pay for change. We were living on our last few dollars. This experience taught me that we are all on a fixed income, unless someone is printing his own money. The only difference in economic social classes is that some people are one check from the poorhouse and others are just a few checks away.

The next morning, with the persistence and drive to find another opportunity, I continued searching for positions on the internet. I learned about an annual networking and career expo conference a company was having at a nearby hotel. The conference was that same day, and I was determined to attend.

I told my wife and kids about it, and scraped up the last $1,500 dollars from my savings account to attend. Once I arrived at the conference and entered the hotel lobby area, I noticed a business meeting occurring in one of the dining rooms. I recognized Mike Lewis, the vice president of one of my prior company's competitors. With the ambition of a lion trying to catch a meal, I decided to approach him to see if I could land a position in his company, Spencer Enterprises.

I had my fifteen-second elevator speech ready to go. As their meeting concluded, people began to exit the dining room walking in my direction. Reaching out my hand and calling his name I said, "Lewis, how are things going? I am on the market and would be interested in talking with you about opportunities in your organization."

He replied obnoxiously from too much to drink, "If it isn't old JOE BRAXTON." He made a sarcastic comment and said loudly to all his peers standing around him, "Let me introduce you to the man that single-handedly took down McBracey Enterprises."

One of his colleagues asked, "Well, great, who did he work for?" And Lewis replied hysterically laughing, "McBracey Enterprises. He took out his own company." They all walked out of the hotel in a roar of laughter.

Embarrassed, I turned to walk away thinking suicide was the only way to stop the pain, but as I headed toward the back of the hotel, Brad Spencer, the CEO of Spencer Enterprises, was standing before me. I recognized him because I had just seen him on the cover of *Future* magazine.

He said, "Let me apologize for my team's behavior; they have had a pretty good year and we are celebrating our fourth quarter results, so I apologize if they were out of hand."

I responded, "No sir, nothing wrong with a little competitive rivalry." Then Brad asked, "Did I hear Lewis refer to you as Braxton, Joe Braxton?"

I replied yes, thinking he recognized my name from my previous employer. Assuming that experience was what he was interested in, I proceeded to give him my 15-second career and experience pitch while handing him my business card. Clearly he was not interested in my background because he cut me off before I could get my second word out. Looking at my business card, he said "I had a good friend with that same name, but he was James Joseph Braxton.

He leaned closer to me, looking at my eyes and face and said, "You look like him." He asked me if I was related to any Braxtons in North Carolina. I did not answer him immediately because James Joe Braxton was my grandfather, and I initially thought to deny him because I wanted to impress the CEO, and I was embarrassed that my grandfather had died penniless. It was normal for me to mislead and fabricate my relationships to people in order to get ahead.

But this time my Super-Conscience steered me and I stated that James Joe Braxton was my grandfather. Mr. Spencer replied, "Small world. He was a good man, a good rich man!"

I replied, "No sir, my grandfather wasn't a rich man; he died penniless because he gave everything he had away." The CEO said, "I see. Well, take care and nice meeting you." He then turned and walked out the hotel.

I stood confused as he walked away. I thought, you blew it again, Braxton. You should have not mentioned your grandfather. I thought again, maybe Spencer was drinking with the rest of the guys and had me mixed up with someone else. I then turned and went into the conference I had drained my savings account to attend.

Nine
The Richness of a Penniless Man

Two weeks passed. I began to reflect on all of the things I had done over the last several months to find an opportunity. I had called and talked with 10 recruiters at the top recruiting firms in the nation, applied for over 150 positions, interviewed for several, and attended a $1,500 networking and career expo conference. I was motivated and energetic in all of the interviews and in my pursuit for happiness, but I never received replies or callbacks from the recruiters or interviewers.

I started to revert to my old thinking about life. Maybe I was wrong, but the Will in me would not let me give up. I pressed on, calling people and searching for opportunities under every rock.

One morning the telephone rang, and on the line was a recruiter from Spencer Enterprises who said the CEO, Mr. Spencer, whom I had met that night at the hotel wanted to meet with me.

As I walked into the corporate headquarters, I could not help feeling great because I was meeting with the CEO. I wondered how many other people have this opportunity. My confidence was up and I knew I was qualified for any opportunity he wanted to offer me.

I was hungry and eager for a new start. I recited my 4 Point Performance Oath as I walked into the office of the CEO.

1. Follow your conscience, never allowing the resurrection of my Super-Ego.
2. Rebuild my name and credibility for the next generation.
3. Perform at my maximum potential each day as if it were my last.
4. Thank God for each day, for each day is an opportunity to do what I didn't do yesterday!

Sitting outside the CEO's office, I wondered what position he wanted to interview me for. I had applied for several, but the recruiter did not specify which position he wanted to talk about. I thought to myself, did he just fire someone and think of me? Maybe it was all the great things I did while I was at the other companies I worked for. Maybe he heard about how great I was, or, better yet, maybe he was impressed when he met me at the hotel.

The secretary escorted me into the CEO's office.

Before I could say anything, he said in a bass voice, "Have a seat, Braxton." He went on to say, "The only reason why you're sitting in this chair is because of the relationship I had with your grandfather." And he told this story:

"Your grandfather was a good man, a rich man, and he had a good name. He helped me build this company by inspiring me when no one else would."

"You see, when I was in college, your grandfather was the janitor at the university. My last semester of school, when I didn't have the money to pay for tuition, your grandfather was there to help me. I had just returned for my senior year and didn't have any money for the semester. I had exhausted all financial aid and loans. As I tried to register, I was told by the registrar that I had to pay the outstanding balance financial aid would not cover. I sat on a bench with my head in my hands, wondering what I was going to do because I had no mother or father to turn to. They died when I was a young child.

"Your grandfather saw me sitting there and asked me, 'What's wrong, son?' I looked up and saw a 70-year-old man, standing with a push broom in his hand. I put my head back in my hands. He asked again, 'What's wrong?' Thinking he couldn't help, with tears flowing from my eyes, I reluctantly told him I didn't have any money to enter school and needed to pay the balance for my last semester's tuition.

"Your grandfather asked how much I needed. I told him the balance was $5,000, and I didn't know where I could get the money. Your grandfather told me to come with him, and we went over to the registrar's office. Your grandfather took out a loan from the university since he was an employee and arranged deductions from his bi-weekly check to pay off the loan. When I saw him doing this, I said 'No sir, please you don't have to do that.' He replied, 'Pay me back when you can, and if I leave this earth before you can, pass it along to someone else, pass it on.'"

"You see, Braxton, your grandfather did not die penniless; he was a rich man, a rich man in giving and rich in name! During the semester as your granddad cleaned the halls, he would see me sometimes attending and leaving engineering classes. He would see my engineering designs and drawings of buildings, and he would ask, 'What building is that?' I would reply, 'My manufacturing company. I am going to make products and sell them across the world one day.'"

"And your granddad would tell me, 'Well, you better keep your nose to the ground because there are a lot of birds looking for that same worm.' And he would tell me the story about millions of birds, all competitors, waking up and hopping on the ground searching for worms to survive. He would go on to say 50 percent of the birds are eaten by their predators because they do not have enough energy or strength to survive, and 50 percent of the worms die because they are caught by the birds, so it doesn't matter if you are a bird or worm, in the morning you better have your nose to the ground."

"Your granddad would tell that story to me every day. He is one of the reasons I am where I am today. He believed in me just as he did in you. Your grandfather died before I could pay him back, and I lost touch with him and didn't know he had died until I met you that night at the hotel. So, Braxton, since I have not passed his gift on to anyone else, I am going to pass it down to you."

"I am willing to invest in you, Braxton, on behalf of your grandfather and his good name. It is clear to me that your track record is not on your side, but knowing your grandfather leads me to believe that you have the same potential, ethics and dedication that poured out of him. And it is my job to pull it out of you whether you like it or not."

"That said, Braxton, I am not making any promises to you, but I will allow you to interview for the executive vice president position you applied for. I am giving you a shot to work for my team and prove yourself. From here on out, you are on your own, and it will be up to you whether or not you get the job and are successful. And it will be up to you whether or not you keep the job. Braxton, the interview process begins right now. You meet with me first, then with several of my direct reports, and then there will be a final panel interview."

Ten
In Every Opportunity,
"Drop It Like It's Hot"

I was ready. My Super-Conscience led my thoughts. I made the decision when I killed my Super-Ego that I was going to be myself and answer interview questions based on my new philosophy and what I thought, and not on what I thought the interviewer wanted to hear. As the interview progressed, I became more and more comfortable, for I was now my own person. The interview turned from question-and-answer session to an engaging conversation about values, philosophies and life challenges. Against the laws of Interviewing 101, I couldn't run from my track record so I brought it up. The CEO raised concerns about perceptions of me and wondered why I had transitioned between companies in such a short period of time. I shared with him my old philosophy of life and also my out-of-body experience and the lessons I had learned as a result. He listened passionately to my new views and philosophies and thanked me for sharing my insights and transformation story.

Interview after interview, I was passionate, enthusiastic and, more importantly, I was authentic, myself, for I had already reached rock bottom and there was nowhere to go but up. Everything was going great until I walked into the next interview office: there behind a huge mahogany executive desk, sat Mike Lewis, the vice president of services, the same person I had the embarrassing encounter with the night I met the CEO of Spencer Enterprises.

As I walked into his office, he just stared at me for 60 seconds as if he were trying to pierce through my confidence. I looked into his eyes to allow him access to my level of desire, for the eyes are the windows into the soul.

After the silence, he looked at me and said sternly, "Braxton, let's get one thing straight. This company does not need a man with your type of reputation. You have job hopped your way up the corporate ladder. I despise you and you make us all look bad. You are not committed. Your record is against you, and I'm going to do everything in my power to make sure you do not get this job! Is that understood?" he exclaimed.

I replied, "Yes, Mike, that is understood. But just know one piece of information before you make your decision. Being fired and resigning from McBracey Enterprises was the best thing that ever happened to me. It gave me an opportunity to look at myself in the frame and I didn't like the picture I saw. It gave me a new perspective on life."

"You see, sometimes we cannot see how we are living our lives because we are consumed by the frame itself. We are too close to the picture. It is hard to see what we have turned into."

"And sometimes you need something to knock you out of the frame so you can see yourself. That is what getting fired from McBracey Enterprises did for me. It allowed me the opportunity to look deep into the frame, and I didn't like what I saw. So I changed my philosophy of life. I explained to him that life is about four things:

- Life is now about performing at your maximum potential
- Never letting your ego dictate decisions for you
- Delivering value each day as if it were your last
- Using each day as a gift to complete what you didn't get done yesterday

"Mike, I have been fortunate enough to step out of the frame and relive my career and decisions. And I have come to the following conclusions: Yes, I have not been challenged. Yes, I was a slacker. Yes, I have not performed to my maximum potential. And, yes, I could have done more in one year than I have done in the last ten years. The difference between me and the other candidates is that I have had an encounter with my Super-Ego and my Super-Conscience and won the battle. I am now a changed person, the question is, who and what are you hiring in the other candidates?"

In that moment, Mike Lewis concluded the interview.

Eleven
Storms of Opportunity

The following Saturday I went out to the mailbox and when I pulled out the mail, I saw a letter from Spencer Enterprises. Eagerly, I opened it and found an offer to join Spencer Enterprises as the Executive Vice President of Business Services, competing head-to-head in the same market as McBracey Enterprises.

I told my wife and kids and they were ecstatic! I quickly accepted the offer. When the Human Resources recruiter asked me when I could start, I replied, "tomorrow."

I reported to work the next day and put together a 90-day transition plan. I presented the plan to the CEO, Mr. Spencer, and he approved it. I moved forward with a sense of urgency and a commitment level I didn't know I had.

After my third week on the job, I learned that Mike Lewis was the only person on the interview team who had not supported hiring me. My first goal was to get him on my side by building a relationship of trust. I made it a strategic goal for us to work on projects together in order to improve our relationship. Over the course of several months, Mike and I became strong supporters of one another and, more importantly, friends.

After mastering my 4 Point Performance System, I had a run of five years performing at my maximum potential and received stellar performance reviews, awards and industry recognitions.

Spenser Enterprises became the number one leader in the market and began acquisition analysis to increase business growth by acquiring competitors. I was selected to head up the acquisition analysis team, a promotion that required my reporting directly to the CEO and President, Brad Spenser. After months of planning and development, I presented the business case for the acquisition of several competitors; one of them was McBracey Enterprises, my previous employer. After receiving board approval, Spenser Enterprises acquired McBracey Enterprises.

During the year after the acquisition, there were several reorganizations and realignments. Given the structural changes, all of the executives had to reapply and contend for their positions. After a series of interviews over a six-month period, I was promoted to President and CEO of McBracey and Spenser Enterprises. Mrs. Jackie Johnson and Mik Lewis now report to me.

"Thank you for firing me; it was the best thing that could have ever happened to me."

Conclusion

When Joe Braxton got fired from McBracey Enterprises by his new boss, Mrs. Jackie Johnson, failure, gloom and dismay pushed Braxton and his family to the lowest point in their lives. Despair forced Braxton to discover the battle was not between him and McBracey Enterprises but rather between his Conscience and Super-Ego. Once he came to this realization, the worst thing he thought could ever happen to him was, in fact, the best thing that ever happened to him. Getting fired by Mrs. Jackie Johnson forced Braxton to unleash his Super-Conscience and take control over his own destiny.

The greatest success in Braxton's life was not when he was shattering all business goals and objectives but when he displayed enough courage to take a look at his life by walking out of the picture frame and realizing he was the major deterrent to his own success.

Braxton's transformation began when he decided to take control over his dreams and aspirations with the help of his Super-Conscience and lessons from his grandfather who helped him battle with his powerful Super-Ego.

The most significant event in Joe Braxton's story was when he was fired, buried his Super-Ego and resurrected his Super-Conscience. In the great words of Napoleon Hill, Braxton was "searching for the magic key that would unlock the door to the source of power within; but yet he had the key in his own hands, and he used the key the moment he learned to control his thoughts." (Napoleon Hill). Braxton's magic key to his life's transformation was hidden within his Will. And once he discovered the key was in his hands to access his Will, the "Will Factor," became the source of his power to overcome the impossible, achieve his dreams and aspirations and perform at his maximum potential! Friends once released the "Will Factor," becomes the key to Overcoming You and making your Dreams A Reality!

This story spans all generations, social classes and cultures. It is a story of the Super-Conscience and Super-Ego that exist in every man, woman, boy and girl. This is a story for anyone who is willing to step out of the picture frame to assess the need for change, making a constructive evaluation of his or her behaviors, accomplishments, family, relationships, health, philosophies, successes and failures in life in order to make life changes which will maximize performance and optimize potential. It is this human process that allows the realization that change is an enabler to success, and storms often foster the change.

The story of Joe Braxton is full of "Vitamins for the Mind." The next chapte are learning Vitamins, consisting of quotes and truths to help you in finding success through your storm.

Vitamins for the Mind

VITAMIN A:
Change is not free; it comes at a cost.

Story Truths:
As we saw with Braxton, change is not free. His change came with a high cost. Sometimes we make decisions that change our lives and sometimes we make decisions that keep us stagnant. Our thoughts, philosophy on life and experiences all shape our decisions and ultimately who we are in life.

As we learned through Braxton's battle to reshape his world, once he was fired by Mrs. Johnson, his success was not in remaking his world, but rather in remaking himself.

Quote:
"As human beings, our greatness lies not so much in being able to remake the world—that is the myth of the atomic age—as in being able to remake ourselves." —Mahatma Gandhi

VITAMIN B:
Storms come like a thief in the night, and when you wake up all your friends are gone.

Story Truths:
When you are on top of your game, your friends, family and associates are all around you. But when you go through a life-challenging storm, very few friends remain in your circle. Braxton's friends vanished when his cash dried up and personal stock value plummeted.

There is an old saying that in life family and friends are in your life for a reason, a season and or a lifetime. As we learned as Braxton changed his perspective on life, he lost all of his friends. But his relationships with those who truly loved him never faltered – his family.

Quote:
"A false friend and a shadow stay around only while the sun shines."
—Benjamin Franklin

VITAMIN C:
Success can be found in the storm but you have to seize the opportunity.

Story Truths:
Our comfort level often limits us from taking advantage of opportunities in life because we fear they may be too risky, too much work, or perhaps we might fail and end up worse off than we were before.

Braxton's story reveals that while he was working for McBracey Enterprises he always had the opportunity to excel and reach greatness, but he was comfortable and risk averse. It wasn't until he joined Spencer Enterprises that he found his opportunity for success when all of the executives had to reapply and interview for their positions because of the McBracey Enterprises acquisition reorganization. It was through his pursuit of opportunity, persistence and faith that he became the President of McBracey Enterprises.

Quote:
"Opportunity is missed by most people because it is dressed in overalls and looks like work." —Thomas Edison

VITAMIN D:
A man is rich according to what he is and what he has done, not according to what he has obtained.

Story Truths:
Braxton's grandfather lived his life serving others which created a good name. There are three types of names for an individual: first, the name of the family; second, the given name; and third, the name you make for yourself. Braxton teaches us through a lesson from Mr. Spencer that if you mess up the name you make for yourself, it is a blessing to be able to fall back on the family name. Braxton was able to fall back on

his grandfather's name because of his values and philosophy on life.

Braxton thought his grandfather died a penniless man because he gave everything he had away, but his grandfather was indeed rich and powerful, not for what he had, but for who he was.

Quote:
"Character is power." —Booker T. Washington

VITAMIN E:
The road to realizing your dreams is paved with challenges.

Story Truths:
From the story of Joe Braxton we learn how to dream through the storm of life's challenges. Braxton taught us that in pursuing our dreams, 80 percent of success comes from just showing up. Braxton showed up every day to find another job. Braxton showed up to find an opportunity in his job to reach greatness. And Braxton showed up to pursue his dream.

Braxton's story is a powerful story that motivates us all to pursue and achieve our dreams by shutting our eyes to impossibilities and realizing, with a mustard seed of faith, we can move mountains. Often we are not successful because we do not Dare to Dream. Braxton's dream of becoming CEO of a company came true. Dare to Dream, Dare to Change, Dare to be Great!

Quote:
"The tragedy of life doesn't lie in not reaching your goal. The tragedy lies in having no goal to reach. It isn't a calamity to die with dreams unfilled, but it is a calamity not to dream. It is not a disgrace to reach the stars, but it is a disgrace to have no stars to reach."
—Benjamin E. Mays

Quote:
"All our dreams can come true, if we have the courage to pursue them."
—Walter Elias Disney

Daily Mini Vitamin Quotes

1. *"If you haven't been fired before, then you haven't started to live."*
   —Robert C. McMillan

2. *"Be a lightning rod for change but when it strikes make sure you have one leg up."* —Robert C. McMillan

3. *"Let nothing stop you from networking, not even death, for people even network at funerals."* —Larry A. McMillan

4. *"If you are the smartest one in your group and they all agree with you on everything, then you need to get some new friends."*
   —Robert C. McMillan

5. *"A patient man rides a donkey."* —Maynard McAlpin

6. *" A no is just a yes waiting to happen."* —Willie Jolley

About the Author

What if we all knew in our own way we could achieve the impossible—
in our lives, our place of work, internally—if we all realized we were
STARs?

The World's Leading Moto-Median — with an attitude that everyone
has potential for success and greatness, Robert C. McMillan has a
unique ability to ignite the STAR within organizations, teams and people
unleashing their maximum potential to achieve remarkable results.

A former Professional Comedian/Entertainer, performing with **Sinbad,
from the Bill Cosby Show**, today Robert is characterized as a leading
force in the Professional Speaking industry by his unique story telling
ability and dynamic life-changing presentations. Robert's unique style of
communication, Fortune 500 corporate experience and instant connection
with the audience initiates readiness for change, followed by action.
As a Professional Speaker, Life Coach and Author, he has a passion to
motivate and inspire others to:

- **Overcome the impossible, "Do What They Say Can't Be Done;"**
- **Reach their maximum potential in life;**
- **and achieve their personal and business dreams.**

Robert has developed a series of short story books called, **"Vitamins
For The Mind,®"** that specifically provide strategies and best practices
to overcome life challenges in the form of fictional and non-fictional
stories that are transparent, applicable and easily transferable to
everyone's life. The strategies and tips for life success are illuminated
in the stories making it a fun environment to be entertained, motivated,
inspired and educated all at the same time. "Vitamins For The Mind,®"
will change your life!

Today, a Speaker, Life Coach, Author and Executive Corporate
Businessman, Robert's powerful messages transcend generations,
cultures and management levels. His engaging and humorous
communication style motivates and inspires individuals to reach
for the STARs in business and in their personal lives, no matter the

More about the Author

obstacles, challenges or mountains in front of them. A recognized business leader, Robert uses his wit to challenge, coach and teach corporations, organizations, teams and individuals how to move mountains in processes, people and competition, resulting in improved personal and business performance, products and profits. Robert lives what he motivationally speaks and writes about, he is currently one of the highest ranking minority Senior Executives of one of the world's largest global healthcare company's based in Washington, DC.

As a Life Coach and speaker to corporations and organizations, Robert speaks from his own personal and corporate life experiences working in Corporate America for over eighteen8 years among some of the world's most respected Fortune 500 Companies and Business Leaders, such as Motorola, General Electric, BellSouth, Discovery Channel, Price Waterhouse Coopers, IBM, UBS Paine Webber, Ernst and Young, Cap Gemni, BP AMOCO, Disney and many others. His two recent books *Overcoming You!* and *Dream to Live – Live To Dream*, are guiding STARs for people who want to take control over their destiny to reach their Dreams!

As a result of his commitment to give back, and provide motivation and inspiration to the next generation of leaders, Robert founded the **Circles of Dreams Foundation,**® **INC**. A non-profit organization that provides training, empowerment, scholarships, mentorship, dream job opportunities, motivation and a social network, to help Dreams become a reality, for the next generation of Dreamers – diversified disadvantaged children, youth, teens and adults who dare to Dream but need support from those who are already living similar Dreams – Dream Makers. The Circles of Dreams Foundation® has a three way win- win- win life changing formula, and reduces dependence on social welfare and creates economic stimulus by connecting:

- **Dreamers to Dreamers;**
- **Dreamers to DreamMakers;**
- **and DreamMakers to DreamMakers**.

More about the Author

Please visit www.circlesofdreams.com and join as an individual member, or donate as a Corporate Sponsor/Partner to assist us in making dreams become a reality!

Robert has obtained over eighteen years of Corporate America experience and is a certified professional speaker and member of the NSA (National Speakers Association). He holds a B.S. degree in Finance, MBA, M.S. in Business and has obtained additional certifications: Certified Internal Auditor (CIA), Certified Internal Controls Auditor (CICA), Chief Audit Executive (CAE), Six Sigma Blackbelt and Project Management.

Website and Contact Information:
www.robertcmcmillan.com
www.vitaminsforthemind.info
www.circlesofdreams.com
email: robert@robertcmcmillan.com

Business Contact Information:
The McMillan Group, LLC
P.O. Box 249
Highland, Maryland 20777
1(866) 442-1381

www.ingramcontent.com/pod-product-compliance
Lightning Source LLC
Chambersburg PA
CBHW050914120626
46552CB00004B/1572